The Windows of My World

Copyright © 2011

All rights reserved. No part of this book may be used or reproduced by any means, graphic, electronic, or mechanical, including photocopying, recording, taping or by any information storage retrieval system without the written permission of the publisher except in the case of brief quotations in critical articles and reviews or fair use for academic purposes.

You can order your own copy of this book online at

http://www.cheapercheepercopy.com/bookstore

ISBN - **9780986873034**

Published in Canada by Cheaper Cheeper Copy Inc.

Printed in the United States of America

Cheaper Cheeper Copy, Inc.
800 Rosser Avenue, Unit A1-A
Brandon, MB R7A 6N5
204-717-1487

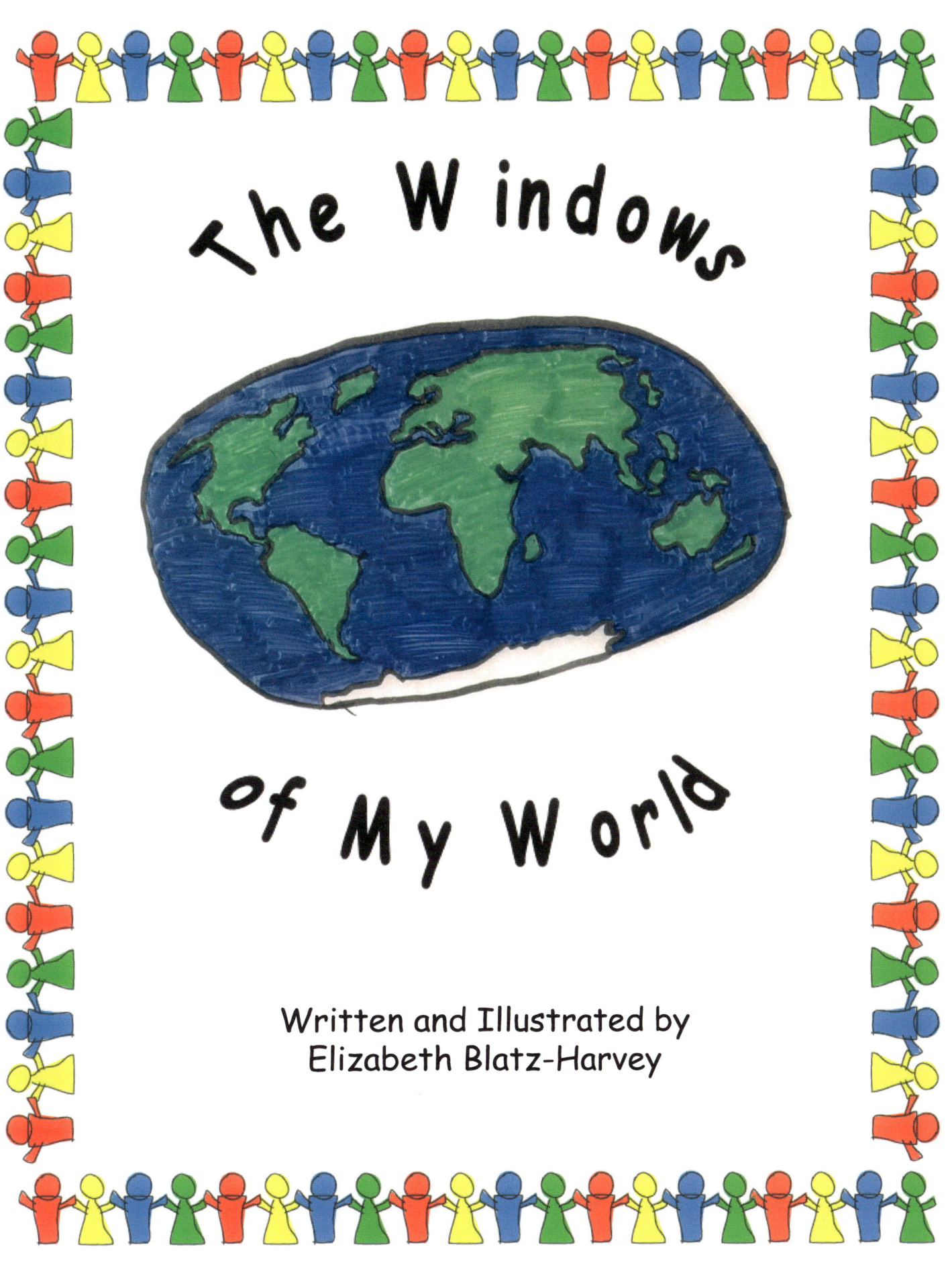

Dedicated to my Niece, Robin Blatz

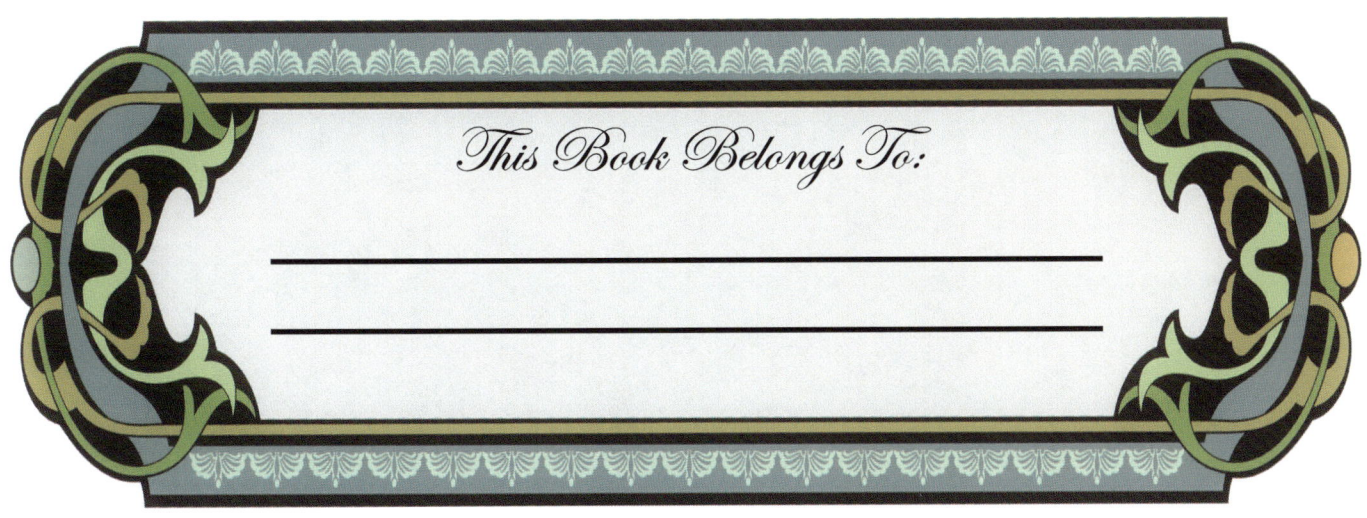

The Windows to Imagination

The Windows to Imagination

Away I go beyond the stars
to a world all full of dreams.
Horror, mystery and adventure are
the stories that I mean.

I curl up in my favourite chair,
a book is in my hands.
I clutch to heart my teddy bear
and soar to far off lands.

When in the mood a horror tale
will chill me to the bone.
Heart beats will race and skin will pale,
I'll wish I was back home.

Suspense will hold a mystery.
I'll dangle by a cliff.
Whatever will the outcome be,
a murder, lie or myth?

But adventure is my favourite,
I'll have the strength of three.
I'll fly, and fight the bad guys,
and the hero I will be.

But all too soon the time is gone.
The book I sadly close.
I have to go to cut the lawn
or write some English poems.

The Windows of My Day

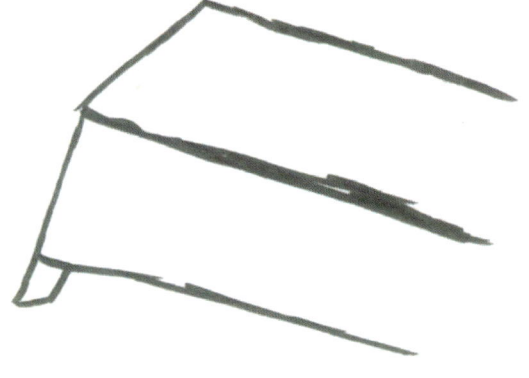

The Windows of My Day

There are many windows in my day.
I look through them and see,
a world plump full of endless life
and possibility.

To learn will help me understand
the world beyond the glass.
To learn will open up the panes,
so now I sit in class.

English, math and writing skills
are things that I must learn,
before I head out on my own
to places that I yearn.

Though spring is bright and sunshine calls,
"Come out to run and play".
I stay and work as best I can
by the windows of my day.

The Window to Their World

The Window to Their World

Black and white and full of grace
the creatures entice me.
I catch a glimpse of another world,
their world below the sea.

As they pass by the steaming glass,
their majesty I see.
But inside their sleek bodies
are minds both sharp and free.

The tricks they do may make us laugh,
but that is not their goal.
Their hope is that they warm our hearts
or maybe touch our souls.

So we can see these creatures
as the royals of the sea,
deserving our respect and love,
deserving to be free.

If we but cherish all the world
both animals and plants,
then the world in turn will cherish us
and all our needs will grant.

The Windows to My World

The Windows to My World

In a car, a plane, a train or boat,
we travel round the globe.
The world we see amazes us.
its colors gaily strobe.

The world is all excitement,
chock full of mystery.
Our understanding only grows
the more we strive to see.

With every mile we journey on
things stay the same or change.
The differences we notice first
when onward we do range.

But the more we take the time to learn,
to listen and to see,
the more we notice likenesses
that bind humanity.

The windows of our vehicle
are like pages in a book.
And travel is the volume.
So take the time to look!

The Window to My Soul

The Window to My Soul

I feel all warm and safe
behind the tall arched panes.
Colors fill the jewelled church windows
as the morning sunshine wanes.

The church is where I sit
to see though to my soul,
to learn to love and cherish all,
to make my body whole.

The comfort, love, compassion there
fill needs that all men feel.
And though religions there are many,
all have the power to heal.

Believe whatever makes you strong
and brings kindness to all others.
For to this world and all its creatures,
we are but token mothers.

About the author:

Elizabeth Blatz-Harvey was born in Winnipeg, Manitoba. She moved to Brandon where she attended Meadows School. After moving to the Tarbolton district she attended Rivers Elementary School and Rivers Collegiate. She graduated from Brandon University with a degree in Elementary Education.

Elizabeth did her training and taught at Mary Montgomery School in Virden, Kenton Elementary School, Deerboine Colony and Riverview School in Brandon. After graduating she did substitute teaching in the area.

Elizabeth's main loves were animals and children.

Elizabeth Blatz-Harvey
1975-2001

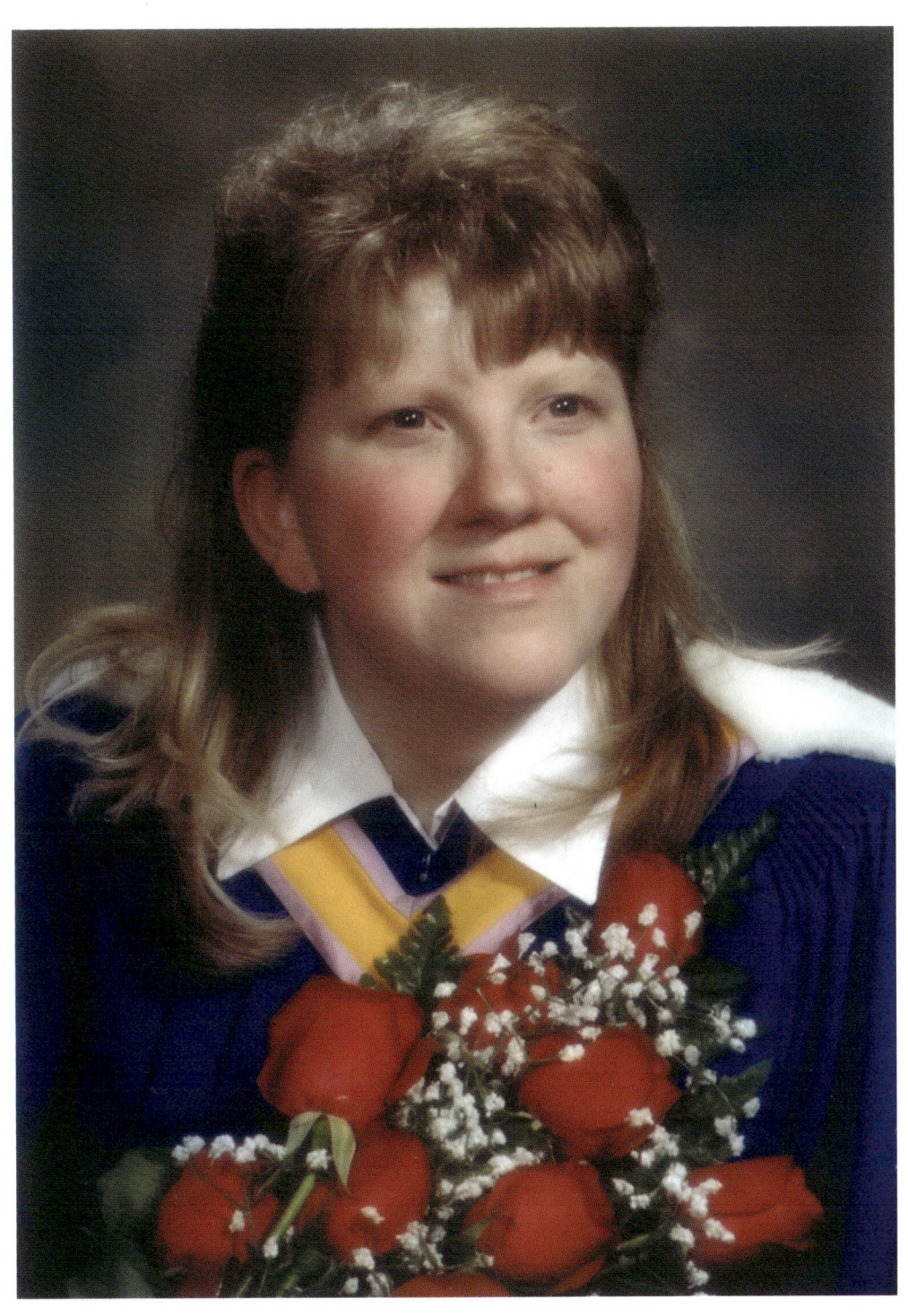

Elizabeth Blatz-Harvey

1975-2001

Elizabeth and Flag

With love from Elizabeth and Flag

CPSIA information can be obtained
at www.ICGtesting.com
Printed in the USA
236263LV00001B